First Day Stories

Katherine K. Newman

Table of Contents

First Day Stories, Copyright 2016 by Katherine K. Newman

Twelve stories about contemporary Quaker life for 3- to 6-year-olds in First Day Schools of unprogrammed Friends Meetings.

ISBN 978-1-365-33377-4 (paperback)

Available in hardback from Lulu.com (no ISBN)

1 2 3 4 5

Preface

In years of teaching First Day School I've often looked for children's stories about contemporary Friends' meeting life and seldom found any; hence my attempts to write them myself.

The stories in this book concern situations familiar to young children who attend meeting. Some focus on the customs and practices of Friends Meetings, for example, shaking hands at the close of worship, holding others in the Light, working at the meetinghouse, or visiting a sick Friend. Others involve problems common to childhood, such as feeling lonely, frustrated, or angry, or wanting possessions that parents won't permit. Every story includes a scene in meeting for worship; the purpose is to help children understand what occurs during that time when everyone sits together quietly. The stories are short enough to allow for other First Day School activities such as discussion, crafts, singing, and play.

My appreciation extends to several Friends: to Carl Magruder for a conversation that nudged me to begin; to Frances Taylor and John Shefelbine for reading drafts and giving suggestions; to William Olling, Henry Olling, and Elizabeth Bell for technical expertise; to Denise MacLachlan and Elizabeth Bell for costuming assistance; to Krista Faries for proofreading; and to Scott Olling for his expert and cheerful formatting.

Katherine K. Newman
Sacramento Friends Meeting
July 2016

Shaking Hands

This is a story about a girl named Hannah. She lived with her grandma, her grandpa, and her brother Jack. They had one dog and one cat, but no fish.

On Sunday mornings Hannah went with her family to
Friends Meeting. Everyone sat quietly in the big room.

At the end of worship, people shook hands with each other and said hello.

Hannah liked to shake hands. She shook hands with people she knew, and she shook hands with people she didn't know.

One day there was a new man at Meeting. His name was Alex. Hannah tried to shake hands with him, but he didn't shake hands with her. He didn't say hello.

The next week Hannah didn't go over to Alex. She
didn't say good morning to him. She shook hands with
others but not with him.

Hannah's grandma asked her, "Why didn't you shake hands with Alex?"

Hannah said, "I tried, but he didn't shake hands with me."

"Alex can't hear very well," said Grandma, "so he probably didn't hear you. He can't see very well, so he probably didn't see you. Touch his hand. Say good morning in a loud voice."

Hannah went over and stood in front of Alex. She felt a little scared, but she reached out and touched his hand. Alex held out his hand and said, "Good morning, good morning! Who are you and how are you?"

Hannah answered in a loud voice. "I'm Hannah, and I'm fine."

"I'm very glad to shake hands with you," Alex said, "very glad indeed!"

From that day on, Hannah shook hands with Alex every week.

The End

Frisky Gets Sick

    This is a story about a boy named Jack. He lived with his grandma, his grandpa, and his sister Hannah. They had one dog and one cat, but no fish.

The dog was named Frisky, and he was very frisky. He chased Jack, and Jack chased him. They loved to roll on the floor together.

One day Frisky was sick, and Grandpa took him to the vet. When they came home, Grandpa laid Frisky gently on his rug.

Then he spoke to Jack and Hannah. "The vet said that Frisky needs to rest. So no chasing, no rolling around, no frisking until he gets better."

All that day Jack felt sad that he couldn't play with Frisky. Frisky just lay quietly on his rug.

After supper Jack really wanted to play. He forgot what
Grandpa said. Soon Jack was chasing Frisky around the
room.

All of a sudden, Frisky dropped down and just lay
there. He didn't move. Jack was scared. "Grandpa, I think
Frisky's dead!"

Grandpa came in from the kitchen. "I'd better take him
back to the vet," he said.

After a long time Grandfather brought Frisky home and
laid him on his rug.

"Come here, Jack," he said. "Frisky was supposed to
rest, but you made him play. Now he's worse. We need to
take good care of him."

Sunday morning Jack went to Meeting with his family. He sat with everyone in the quiet room. He was sorry that he had made Frisky sicker. Deep in his heart he said, "I won't do that again."

The End

Jack Feels Lonely

Jack and Hannah lived with their grandma and grandpa.
They had one dog and one cat, but no fish.

One Saturday Grandpa and Grandma had to take
Hannah to an appointment.

Allison, a Friend from Meeting, stayed with Jack.

It was raining, so they couldn't go to the park. First they
played cars.

Then they played block towers.

Jack liked Allison, but it seemed like a long time since his family had left. Jack felt lonely and wished they would come home.

Jack thought about how he and Grandpa liked to brush
Frisky together. He thought about how Grandma let him
help cook supper.

Jack thought about Hannah, too. She liked to tease him,
but they often had fun together.

Finally Jack heard the front door open. They were
home! Grandpa and Grandma gave him a hug. Hannah
said, "Hey, Jack." Jack was glad to have them back.

The family went to Meeting on Sunday morning and sat together. The room was very quiet. Jack thought about yesterday. He felt thankful for his family.

The End

Holding in the Light

Every Sunday Hannah and Jack went to Friends Meeting with their family. Near the end of worship the clerk said, "If you would like us to hold someone in the Light, say their name." Then people in the meeting said names.

One Sunday night at bedtime Hannah asked Grandma, "Why did we hold Charles in the Light?"

Grandma said, "Because he's in the hospital."

"Why did we hold Emily in the Light?"

"She graduated from high school. We're glad for her."

"Who is Benjamin? Why did we hold him in the Light?"

"Benjamin is in prison, and his brother asked us to hold him in the Light."

Hannah asked, "What does 'hold in the Light' mean?"
Grandma said, "When we hold someone in the Light, we remember how the love of God is always around them."

Grandma turned the light off. "If we forget that God is near us, it's like being in the dark. We can't see where we're going."

She turned the light on again. "When we remember that God is with us, it's like having the light on."

"Good night, sweetheart," Grandma said. "I hold you in the Light every day."

"Why?" asked Hannah.

"Because I love you," replied Grandma.

The End

Workday at the Meetinghouse

Jack lived with his grandma, his grandpa, and his sister
Hannah. They had one dog and one cat, but no fish.

One Saturday morning Jack went with Grandpa and Grandma to the meetinghouse for a workday. Chris showed everyone the list of jobs for the day.

Grandpa took a spray bottle and cloth to wash the
windows.

Grandma went to clean tables in the classroom.

Daniel wanted to plant flowers.

Marian said she would rake the dead leaves.

Bill swept the sidewalk.

Jack helped Chris for a while.

Then Jack went into the worship room and set up some roads and bridges.

He stopped playing for a minute and looked around. He thought about Sunday mornings when so many Friends would sit here in quiet worship. The room felt peaceful now, too.

The End

When Hannah Felt Angry

This is a story about Hannah. She lived with her
grandma, her grandpa, and her brother Jack. They had one
dog and one cat, but no fish.

Hannah had a friend named Jasmine next door, and she
played with Jasmine every day.

One day Hannah wanted to play with the wagon.

"May I play with your wagon?" asked Hannah.

Jasmine said, "No, not now."

Hannah said, "Please?"

Jasmine said, "No."

Hannah said, "That's not fair."

Jasmine said, "I don't care."

Hannah went home. She was upset. The next day
Grandma said, "Do you want Jasmine to come over today?"

"No, I don't," said Hannah. Hannah played alone that
day, but it wasn't much fun. She missed Jasmine, but she
still felt angry.

On Sunday Hannah's family went to Meeting. Everyone sat quietly in worship. Hannah thought about Jasmine. Hannah was still angry. But after a while the anger went away. She didn't feel angry any more. She just felt peace and love in the meeting.

After Meeting Hannah told her grandmother, "I want to play with Jasmine again." Grandma gave her a big hug.

The End

The Woman Who Cried

On Sundays Jack went with his family to Friends Meeting.
Everyone sat quietly in the big room. It was peaceful.

One day during Meeting Jack heard someone crying.
He looked around. The person who was crying was a
grown-up named Susan. Jack was surprised to see a
grown-up cry.

Jack whispered to his grandmother, "Why is Susan crying?"

Grandma whispered back, "I will tell you after Meeting."

Jack watched Susan. The woman next to her gave her a hug. Soon Susan stopped crying. The meeting was still for a long time.

After Meeting several people spoke to Susan.

"Susan's mother died yesterday," Grandma told Jack. "The meeting was holding Susan in the Light. And now Friends are talking with her and telling her they are sad that her mother died."

Jack looked at Susan. Susan was almost smiling now.

The End

A Walk

Hannah lived with her grandma, her grandpa, and her brother Jack. They had one dog and one cat, but no fish. One day Grandpa and Hannah went for a walk.

"It feels good to be alive!" said Grandpa.

Hannah took a deep breath. The air smelled so fresh.

"Close your eyes and listen," said Grandpa.

Hannah closed her eyes and listened.

"Birds are singing!" she said.

"Look at this," said Grandpa. Hannah opened her eyes.
Grandpa was pointing to a bright yellow flower.

Hannah kneeled down and smelled it. "Mmmm."

Sunday morning Hannah went to Meeting with her
family. She sat still with everyone in the big room. Hannah
thought about fresh air and birds and flowers. She said
a silent prayer: "Dear God, Thank you for this beautiful
world. Love, Hannah."

The End

Uncle's Dog

This is a story about Hannah and Jack. They lived with their grandma and grandpa. They had one dog (Frisky) and one cat (Cat-Cat), but no fish.

One day Grandma told them that Uncle's dog Rocky was coming for a week because Uncle was going on a trip.

When Rocky arrived, Jack tried to take him for a walk,
but he wouldn't stand still to have the leash put on.
Hannah tried to hug him, but he wouldn't let her.
Instead he started chasing Cat-Cat.

Rocky barked and barked.

He tried to nip Grandpa's ankles.

He ate Frisky's food.

He wouldn't let Frisky sleep on his own rug.

Frisky hid under the bed and wouldn't come out.

Finally Uncle came for Rocky. He and Grandma had a talk.

"You need to take Rocky to obedience school," she
said. "We can't have him here again until you do."

"Yes, that's probably a good idea," replied Uncle.

Finally Uncle and Rocky left. Frisky came out from
under the bed. He and Jack rolled around on the floor.

"Well," said Grandpa, "Having Rocky was not pleasant
for us, but we wanted to help Uncle, and we did."

Meeting on Sunday felt very peaceful after a week
with Rocky. Jack thought about what Grandpa had said.
Sometimes helping isn't fun, but we do it anyway.

Grandpa said a silent prayer: "Thank you, God, for our
patience."

The End

Visiting Sara

One Sunday in First Day School, Richard, the teacher, said that Sara Ramirez was home in bed. Everyone knew Sara, because she used to be their teacher. The class made get-well cards.

Jack, Hannah, and Grandma took the cards to Sara.
They made a pot of soup and took flowers, too.

Sara smiled when she saw them. "I'd love to see your cards," she said.

She handed Jack a control. "Would you press the top button?"

The upper part of the bed went up, and Sara was sitting up.

"Hannah, your turn. Press the button on the bottom,"
said Sara.

Hannah pressed, and the mattress bent under Sara's knees.

"I wonder who invented this bed," said Grandma.

"Whoever they are, I'm grateful to them," said Sara.

The next Sunday Jack was sitting in Meeting for Worship. He thought about Sara's movable bed. He hoped that someday he could invent something that people would be thankful for.

The End

Simplicity

This is a story about Hannah. She lived with her
grandma, her grandpa, and her brother Jack. They had one
dog (Frisky) and one cat (Cat-Cat), but no fish.

One day Hannah was daydreaming about tropical fish
she had seen in the pet store. Their colors were so pretty.
She loved to watch them swim.

"Grandma," she asked, "Can we get some tropical fish?"

Grandma thought for a minute. Then she said gently,

"No, that's not a good idea for us."

"Why?" asked Hannah.

"It's a matter of simplicity," said Grandma. "First, we already have Frisky and Cat-Cat. They are wonderful. We don't need too many pets."

"Second," said Grandma, "tropical fish would cost
money. We don't need to spend too much money."

Sunday in Meeting a woman named Elena stood up
to give a message: "I've been thinking about simplicity.
Sometimes I buy too many things, and then I think too
much about what I bought. When that happens it's hard to
remember God's love."

Hannah thought about Frisky and Cat-Cat. They were a lot of fun. Maybe having them was enough.

The End

Christmas Stockings

One Sunday in First Day School, Richard, the teacher,
talked about people who did not have homes.
"It's hard for them in the winter," he said.

The class discussed what people need in winter.

"Hats. Gloves. Jackets. Socks. Food. Hot drinks," said the children.

"We can fill Christmas stockings with some of these things," said Richard.

Grandma and Jack went shopping. They came home
with bags full of socks, gloves, lip balm, shoelaces, soap,
and gift cards.

Several Friends in Meeting knitted warm hats.

The class filled the stockings. They put in toothbrushes,
toothpaste, tissues, and the things that Jack and Grandma
had bought.

There was a knitted hat at the top of each stocking.

"We'll show these during announcements after Meeting for Worship," said Richard.

Hannah wondered who would receive the stocking
she filled. She tried to hold that person in the Light even
though she didn't know who it would be. She hoped that
the person would have a home soon.

The End